Willy Runs Away

by Anne Rockwell

E. P. DUTTON   NEW YORK

Library of Congress Cataloging in Publication Data

Rockwell, Anne F.   Willy runs away.

SUMMARY: An adventurous dog runs away from home only to find
the world isn't as pleasant and attractive as he imagined.
[1. Dogs—Fiction   I. Title.]
PZ7.R5943Wi [E]   77-16417   ISBN 0-525-42795-3

Published in the United States by E. P. Dutton, a Division
of Sequoia-Elsevier Publishing Company, Inc., New York

Published simultaneously in Canada by Clarke,
Irwin & Company Limited, Toronto and Vancouver

Editor: Ann Durell   Designer: Riki Levinson
Printed in the U.S.A.   First Edition
10 9 8 7 6 5 4 3 2 1

for Hannah,
Elizabeth,
Oliver

Once there was a little dog named Willy. He had a foxy face, but the rest of him looked like a street-colored mop. He had a cocky, dancing tail and prancing toes.

Willy had four people. He had a good house with a backyard to play in, and a kitchen to eat in, and a corner to sleep in. Near Willy's house was the wide world. Here big, brave dogs roamed, cats hunted, and cars drove fast down the avenue. But Willy was not allowed into the wide world alone without a leash, for he was small and street-colored, and cars drove fast.

Willy's people built a fence for his backyard and told him to stay there. The fence was high and strong. But Willy could dig. One day, when no one was looking, he dug right under his fence and went roaming in the yard next door.

His people came to fetch him, but when they called, he ran off. He thought that was fun. Then his people came in the beautiful blue car, and because Willy liked to ride in the beautiful blue car, he jumped in. He rode all the way home from the yard next door. He liked that.

"Willy can dig too well," said Willy's man, and then the people put heavy bricks, and stones and logs, all along the fence. And so Willy could not dig.

But he could climb. And late one afternoon, when some big, brave dogs came running by, Willy tiptoed right over the fence.

He ran with the big, brave dogs all afternoon.
And then they all went home for their suppers.
But Willy did not go home. He was lost, alone,
and far, far from home.

But he could sniff. "Sniff, sniff," he sniffed all the way to the school where his boy and girl went. But his boy and girl were not there, and the school was dark and closed.

"Sniff, sniff," went Willy, to the sailboat pond
in the park, but no one was there. A raccoon
hissed at Willy, and showed his white teeth. Willy
was scared, and he ran away.

High rose the moon, and damp dew fell. Willy sniffed past the gas station and to the supermarket, and his people were not there. He could not sniff a friend anywhere.

He lay down in the parking lot and cried. He
did not feel like a big, brave dog, but he did feel
hungry. He could sniff good bones, but they were
all locked up.

At Willy's house his people hunted. They called the neighbors. They called Willy. But Willy could not hear them.

His people cried. They called the dog pound. They called the police. But no one had seen Willy.

In the parking lot, Willy sniffed something he did not like. Rat! Willy slunk off into the night.

But suddenly, "Sniff, sniff!" Willy sniffed his boy! "Sniff, sniff." He followed the scent through the dark night.

Finally he came to his boy's friend's house.
He sat on the back stoop and howled and howled.
The father did not know Willy and he shouted,
"Go home! Go on....Shoo!"

And off into the dark night went Willy. Car
lights came bright and fast down the dark avenue.
And oh, but Willy was scared. How the cars
rushed—big and fast! How bad they smelled!

Willy's people put on their nightclothes and brushed their teeth and went to bed. But no one slept.

So at one o'clock in the morning, Willy's people got into the beautiful blue car and drove off into the dark night. The headlights shone on the street, but they did not shine on street-colored Willy.

Through the shadowy park with the sailboat
pond went the beautiful blue car, but Willy was
not there. He was not anywhere. Not by the

supermarket, not by the gas station, not by the
school. No, he was not anywhere, and Willy's sad,
tired, worried, sleepy people headed home.

And then, on the big avenue where cars went
fast, Willy's people saw something. They did not
see a little dog with a foxy face and a cocky,
dancing tail and prancing toes.

Oh no. They saw a damp little mop, head
down, tail down, sad and chilled. But it was Willy!

Yes, it was! And Willy saw the beautiful blue car going slowly down the avenue where other cars went fast. He ran to it and jumped inside. He licked his people. He rolled upside down. He wagged his poor, tired tail. And Willy's people drove him home in the beautiful blue car,

to supper in his corner and bed in his kitchen.
And they told him never, never to go over or
under that fence again. And I certainly hope he
never did!

ANNE ROCKWELL wrote this story about her own little dog, a mixed cairn terrier and toy poodle. "He can dig like a terrier and, like some poodles, can tiptoe with ease and dispatch over *any* fence. And he does so if we turn our backs. Since he is small and street-colored, this alarms us. Although our 'beautiful blue car' is in fact very old and tired, he will return home only in that!"

The display types are Roberta Outline and Souvenir Light, both film, and the text is set in Bookman Alphatype. The illustrations were drawn in black wash. The book was printed by offset at Halliday Lithographers.